BILLABONG
DREAMING

*Much has recently been revealed about the cultures
of native peoples around the world.
Their simple beliefs and practices have taken on
a trendy allure in societies where daily life
has become frenzied and chaotic.
Modern people are turning to these older cultures
in an attempt to find meaning and validity in
an otherwise bleak existence.
This is good.
There is much to be learned and handed down
through the generations—
it may even be the saving grace of the planet.*

*In writing **Billabong Dreaming,**
my main intention is to stir up a little curiosity
and desire to better understand the ways in which
the older cultures can enhance our own lives.*

Other short fiction by Brian Jones

Crackle with Life
The Gold-n-Quartz Crystal

With the completion of his third book, *Billabong Dreaming,* Brian Jones has reached a level of maturity he has sought for years. His earlier works, *Crackle with Life* and *The Gold-n-Quartz Crystal,* helped shape his writing into a unique style of adventure and philosophy that appears to mix *that which is* with *that which might be.*

Together with his wife and two children, Brian lives on a small farm outside of Nevada City, California, where he maintains a variety of organic vineyards and receives a strong dose of "soil therapy" almost daily.

BILLABONG DREAMING

An Australian Adventure

❖❖

Brian Jones

Pelican Pond

A Pelican Pond Book
Published by Blue Dolphin Publishing, Inc.
P.O. Box 8, Nevada City, CA 95959
Orders: 1-800-643-0765

ISBN: 0-942444-05-1

Library of Congress Cataloging-in-Publication Data

Jones, Brian, 1963–
    Billabong dreaming : an Australian adventure/
    Brian Jones.
        p.   cm.
    ISBN 0-942444-05-1
    1. Wilderness areas—Australia—Fiction. 2. Australian
aborigines—Fiction. 3. Young men—Australia—Fiction.
4. Authorship—Fiction. I. Title.
PS3560.04579B55 1996
813'.54—dc20   96-13446
                                                    CIP

Front Cover Illustration: Jude Bischoff
Cover Design: Lito Castro

Printed in the United States of America
by Blue Dolphin Press, Grass Valley, California

5   4   3   2   1

Introduction

In the late winter of 1993, my wife Barbara, who was four months pregnant at the time, and I travelled five weeks along the east coast of Australia. Although we both read as much local information and talked to as many people as was possible, I am sure there are a lot of complexities we still have yet to learn about this intriguing land down under.

I am intrigued mainly by the Australian Aborigine people themselves as well as their Dreamtime concept. The idea that a mythological songline can guide a person on the course of their present-day life is a fascination to me. In the truest sense it is the practice of looking at our past to find answers for our future. It is a practice capable of transcending cultural and societal boundaries.

In this book, *Billabong Dreaming,* characters from distinctly different backgrounds come together in a Dreamtime sequence to reveal a common link that unites us all. Perhaps humanity really does share a racial memory.

Brian Jones
Nevada City, California
December, 1995

Billabong Dreaming

I N THE MID 1970s a woman named Rebecca Rollins moved from Sydney, Australia to a small town called Kuranda, which is on the same continent but more than a thousand miles to the north, in Queensland. At that time Rebecca had just graduated from the university in Sydney with a degree in psychology and an emphasis on the behavioral studies of Australian Aborigines. As Kuranda was close to the tribal territories of the Tjapukai, and with money she obtained through federal grants, she went north to write an essay on the behavior of the Tjapukai.

Twenty years later, in 1994, Rebecca Rollins had long since written that essay for the appreciation of a nearly nonexistent audience. She had applied for more grant money but had not even received a reply from the school board. It didn't matter much to Rebecca, because she had been so taken in by the Tjapukai that she hardly needed the government money to get by. She was young and beautiful, and she disregarded her professional ethics by falling in love with a handsome but older tribal member named Jim. Jim was a popular name for aborigine men of Jim's age.

Jim and Rebecca had a son named Douglas. In 1994 Doug was seventeen years old. Doug grew up in Kuranda, and Kuranda grew up with Doug. The small village that Rebecca had moved to when she graduated had become a boutique-town, a high-priced outlet for the tourist attraction that the aborigine culture had become.

It was a pretty comfortable life for Rebecca, Jim, and Doug. She had a private practice as a therapist and family counselor, but she also had a profitable secondhand store. Strange and rare antique clothing and jewelry made its way in and out of Kuranda, and a lot of it went through Rebecca's store. Jim had taken on more and more of the tribal responsibilities over the years and had become a community leader.

The tourist industry was not altogether bad for Kuranda. It brought a lot of revenue to the area, and it afforded an exchange of cultures. The Tjapukai built a dance theater where they showcased their traditional tribal dances in an attempt to convey their mythology of Dreamtime to the masses that arrived daily on tour buses. Douglas had started dancing for the theater when he was very young and had evolved to become one of their most prominent luminaries.

Around noon on a warm day in January, 1994, Doug was hanging around outside of the theater, already dressed for his performance. He liked to mingle with the audience and feel their appreciation and admiration. Doug noticed a young, white boy who didn't look like he belonged with the tourist crowd. The boy had the look of a hobo about him, a rather hand-to-mouth appearance that spoke of the outback—like one who travels the bushman's fabled tucker track in a perpetual search for the next meal.

"So, how long've you been on the tucker-track?" Doug asked, adjusting his costume loin-cloth and checking his makeup in the theater window.

"Most of my life, it seems," said Billy. "But this time's for good. Ain't goin' back home again 'til I'm a sure 'nough man." He pulled the unsmoked half of a hand-rolled cigarette from his shirt pocket and lit it with a paper match. Holding his vice in the left corner of his mouth, he exhaled the smoke from the other side as though he had been doing it for years.

"How old are you?" asked the tribal dancer, smiling and waving to the tourists as he spoke to the young lad.

"I'm goin' on sixteen in a coupl'a months." Billy withdrew the cigarette butt casually, then spit a piece of tobacco on the sidewalk. He puffed at the remaining embers greedily, slightly burning his fingertips, then tossed the tiniest scrap on the ground and crushed it with a worn-out gym shoe.

"Well," Doug said, "I better get inside before the show starts without me. But if you're still around this afternoon, I'll show you a good place to camp by the river." The dark-skinned dancer took a final glance at his reflection, then strode regally through the crowd gathered around the Tjapukai Dance Theater.

Billy watched him go, and then he watched the faces of the tourists standing in line to buy tickets to the show about the Australian Aborigines. Their eyes widened when they saw the dancer, as though one of the gods had descended amongst them-a god, or else the village idiot, they weren't sure which. They regarded him with awe and curiosity, a mixture one might feel upon encountering an alien being—as though something about him could answer the questions they couldn't even verbalize.

What was it about the Australian Aboriginies that made people from all the other countries so twitchy and nervous?

It was sort of a fascination to Billy—all these people lined up to pay good money to watch these darkfellows dance. Lots of people in line, not just a few. This theater must be making a lot of money, surmised the young lad from a poor family. Maybe it wasn't a mistake to take the ride up here. The driver of the car he had hitched with told him that Kuranda might be a cool place to meet some people, and now, here he was, and he had already met a local celebrity.

The road sure can take some funny turns, he thought, as he walked across the street and into the bakery. For $1.60 he bought a good-sized, fresh-baked vegetable pie which he took around the corner, out of town a ways, to a shady spot beneath a Coolibah tree.

4

Here he threw down his backpack, or "swag," as he preferred to call it in traditional Australian bush terms, and sat down to eat his pie. The meal was quite nice, with a fine, flaky crust and steaming hot vegetables inside. Accompanied by a bit of fresh water from his canteen, the first meal of the day was to his satisfaction.

It was a glorious day to be in the jungles of the Cape York Peninsula in far northern Queensland. The summer weather of this January day was almost perfect—clear, blue skies and warm sunshine, temperature around thirty degrees Celsius, humidity just a little high from last week's early monsoon rain. It would get drier though, just as soon as he got farther south, down into New South Wales.

Billy rolled himself a cigarette and dug around in his swag to find his tattered paperback edition of Henry Lawson's *Collected Short Stories*. Reading was the one benefit Billy had gotten from his brief, over-the-air, radio schooling. Science and math didn't hold much allure for him, except to learn to count the sheep on the station his family took care of. Counting sheep and adding money, which didn't come along too often, and giving the sheep their medicine when they fell sick—these were Billy's only practical applications for math and science. But reading offered an escape from the dull, outback routine of his life. It is no more unusual in the Australian bush than in the mountains of northern California to find a lonely cabin well-stocked with reading material.

Billy's favorite author was Henry Lawson, who wrote in the late 1800s and the turn of the century, and who became a folk hero and symbol of the early Australian colonial days. Henry Lawson and Banjo Patterson were the main reasons Billy had learned to read at all. Ever since his father had read to him as a small child, the wandering, droving tales of Henry Lawson had been a source of inspiration for his imagination.

All through his childhood, as he was growing up working with his four brothers and two sisters on the sheep station, Billy satisfied his curiosity about the outside world through the written works of men he aspired to stand beside. He fancied himself a writer and, though orally his language was that of an outback station hand, when he put his thoughts down on paper, his grammar, punctuation and vocabulary flowed professionally. He attributed this to Lawson, whose influence was undeniable.

Billy wrote, in the form of verse or prose, mainly small stories of ranch life stuffed into a lyric which he could recite and reform as he did his daily work. He wanted to write in a fuller format someday, but his mind was unable to hold its focus very long, and he had to really struggle with dialogue.

He lit his cigarette, opened the pages to his bookmark, and settled in comfortably under the Coolibah tree. The sign on the theater said the last show ended at two that afternoon. He would go meet his new friend after that. But until then, there was nothing pressing him except Lawson's call for literary adventure.

"So, Billy, you're still here. Haven't gotten tired of the tucker-track already, have you?" Doug walked from the back of the theater to meet Billy, who had been waiting in front for more than twenty minutes.

"What's that supposed to mean? You're not makin' fun of me, are you darkfellow?" Billy extended his hand in friendship, and Doug accepted.

"No worries, mate. Just pokin' at you." Doug smiled wide. "Did you see the show?"

"No chance," said Billy. "Haven't got the money."

"Well, it's a good one, I'm one of the lead actors. We tell the story of the creation of Dreamtime. Everyone wants to hear that one. Then we really impress them by making fire." Douglas seemed to believe that Billy was part of an audience and that the show was still on.

"Sounds kind of commercial to me. Guess I just don't understand why everyone is so fascinated by you fellows."

"Where are you from, Billy?" Doug changed the subject.

"Outback. Born on a sheep station along the Saxby River, close to Bunda Bunda. Got six brothers and sisters, and I'm not the oldest or the youngest. Sort of lost in the shuffle, if you know what I mean."

"Yeah, I know what you mean; it's a familiar story in Australia. I bet your papa was a drover, right?"

"Didn't start that way. He was an honest man at first, ran the station well, and even made a profit the first coupl'a years. Then the drought hit an' most the sheep died. That's when he took to the road, tryin' to find work to feed the family. Haven't seen him now for five years."

"What brings you to these parts?" Doug asked, becoming interested in the story.

"Well, after four years of rearin' us children the best she could, my mamma got offered a job mindin' a motel up in Cooktown. So we packed in an' moved up there."

The short, grubby white boy and the uncommonly tall and handsome Tjapukai dancer walked side by side out of Kuranda toward the Mitchell River. They passed the Coolibah tree Billy had rested under earlier that day. It now stood in the exposed heat, the sun having shifted—no longer an inviting shady spot. The heavy heat of the day seemed to oppress everything it beat down upon, making the jungle landscape a dull, green-grey mass with no particular landmarks. Out on the Coral Sea to the northeast, monstrous black thunderclouds marched to the daily rhythm of their evening assault on the hilly, rainforest coastland.

"I didn't care for Cooktown much," Billy continued. "I had never been in a schoolroom before, and all the other kids made fun of me for it. I got most of my education on the Radio Outback, the school channel. Even the darkfellows thought they were better than me. And the tourists, what a silly bunch of gawkers they are. Pouring in day by day in their safari tour buses, pointing at the dark-fellows and taking snapshots. What's the attraction? I felt like we were living in a zoo." Billy scuffed his foot on the ground and watched a few rocks scatter down the hill.

They talked as they walked, and the hill grew steadily steeper. Leaving the final outskirting neighborhood of Kuranda, the unlikely duo came to a trailhead marked by a sign that read "Jungle Trail."

"This is one of our oldest trails," said Doug. "Before we had roads and cars, this was our main route to the river. It goes past the giant waterfall where all the tourists go. That's why we put this sign here, so that people from the city could enjoy a nice walk through a rainforest. We'll use the trail now to get down to the billabong."

"Boy, you're really into this whole tourist thing, aren't you?" Billy said, shifting his pack and tightening the belly band.

"I believe it's important for our two cultures to learn to respect one another, and that one of the ways to do that is through song and dance, as well as hands-on experience, like walking down a jungle trail."

"Damn, Doug, you sound like a politician. You might be good at that. Might ought'a make a career out of it."

Green and orange parrots flew, squawking overhead, warning the other jungle creatures that humans were on the trail. Massive vines dangled from the lofty heights of the Blue Gum trees as cascading water, splashing from rock to rock, mingled with the sounds of chirping insects and shrieking birds. Quietness and solitude would not be found in this densely inhabited jungle.

"I'll show you a place where you can camp. The water is good, and there is plenty of wood around to build a fire. After I have dinner with my parents, I'll try an' bring you some grub. Then we can sit by the fire and talk."

The two boys had taken a side trail that branched off and continued downhill, avoiding the scenic overlook of the waterfall. Not many people used this trail, but it was kept somewhat clear of brush by the locals who used it to go swimming in the billabong. A strip of sandy beach bordered by volunteer sugarcane lay along the banks of the muddy, brown river.

"I wouldn't drink the water this time of year; it's too muddy from the rain and runoff. But there are a couple of clear water springs that make this brackish estuary a true billabong. A lot of wildlife will show up later for their evening drink."

"I've hung around billabongs before. I know what to expect—lots of mosquitoes after the day cools off."

"Very well then, sounds like you'll do fine on your own. If you stay on this side of the river and follow along the southwestern shore, you'll find one of those springs. I'll see you later."

"All right, Doug. Thanks a heap. See you to-night, yeah?" Billy put his hand out to shake, but Doug had already turned to leave. Darkfellows are a strange breed, thought Billy as he watched the lithe, young native move gracefully through the jungle.

Billy kept to the southwestern shore of the coffee-with-milk colored river. The ground had leveled out considerably, and now the water sought its course in multiple directions, spreading out into the jungle to create a very swampy estuary.

Gumtrees clung to the banks in a desperate struggle for survival, growing in a bent and twisted fashion to avoid the threatening water. Coolibah trees gave up the struggle and lay haphazardly strewn along the banks, partly submerged in the relentless current. Billy picked his way through, over and around these fallen sentinels, also avoiding the water's edge as much as possible, with both eyes always on the lookout for alligators and crocodiles.

When he came to the spring, he was well above the sandy bank of the river, scrambling amongst the twisted roots of fallen trees. Expecting the spring to be a typical, small stream that he could step across, he was surprised and almost missed the clear, cold water as it issued forth from the hill itself, mostly hidden by a fallen tree. If it hadn't been for the sound of the small, trickling waterfall, he might have walked right past.

Only one other time had Billy actually seen the source or wellspring of a waterway, far out in the dry, rocky hills around Bunda Bunda. He and his father and his oldest brother Richard had gone out in the Jeep to look for some sheep that had wandered off the station. They had driven around the desert all day, roughly following the Saxby River into the foothills. His father was about to switch on the lights and turn around toward home when they crested a small hill and looked down into a lush, green oasis. The sheep were there, along with a handful of the neighbors' sheep that had been missing more than a week.

Billy's father used the radio to call home and tell the rest of the family that it was too late and too far to go, so they would bring the sheep back in the morning. This had excited Billy more than anything he could remember. He had never spent the night away from home.

Now, as he stood beside the wellspring trickling into the billabong, he could remember that night very well: how he and his brother Richard, with whom he had never been very close, had explored that small creek as they searched for firewood in that other-worldly oasis. They had hiked together for the first time and had come to a place much the same as the spot where he now stood—a place where the water actually sprang free of the hillside and spilled its essence above the ground for the nourishment of living creatures.

Billy had been fascinated, and, even now, that day and night they had spent camping under the stars in the tiny oasis was one of the happiest things he could remember.

An early-rising mosquito, braving the heat of the day, circled once around Billy's head, then landed discretely on the back of his neck. The boy heard the buzzing insect in a distant sort of way, but he didn't pay much attention until he felt the penetration. He slapped the tiny bug with four fingers and smeared his own blood across his neck. The action brought Billy back into the present moment.

"'magine them buggers'll be pretty thick down in this swamp," the boy said aloud. "Better build a fire an' smoke 'em out."

Billy climbed up the bank next to the spring and poked around looking for a comfortable spot. He wanted to be a hundred feet or more from the spring and the muddy river where a well concealed croc might slip up on him unaware. The perfect location was supplied by a large, fallen Coolibah tree whose massive trunk shed its skin-like bark in large sheets. He constructed an impromptu, lean-to with the bark to shelter himself from the inevitable evening shower. Leaning his swag under the shelter, he set about gathering a large pile of firewood. When he felt that his supply was sufficient to last through the night, he scooped a shallow indentation in the earth just outside of his lean-to.

After filling his water bottle and his little black boiling pot from the spring, he returned to his shelter and built a small fire. Using rocks to form a cooking platform within the fire, he then put the pan, or "black billy," as it is referred to in the Australian bush, on to boil. He was feeling quite content as he rolled a cigarette and settled in to digest a little of the ageless wisdom of Henry Lawson.

He opened the tattered paperback to a story about a drover's wife, living outback in a weatherboard shanty full of kids. Billy could fully identify with the setting of his own childhood back in Bunda Bunda. In the story, the drover's wife is left for months at a time while her husband is out droving, which was something of a custom in the early colonial days of Australia.

Billy became completely enthralled as the mother of five children defended the family from an Australian Brown snake that had snuck under the floorboards of their shanty. He felt the mother's anguish when night fell, and she forced the children to sleep on the table for fear the snake might come up through the boards while they were unaware. When daybreak came, and the family dog stirred the mother's struggling consciousness into action, she finally succeeded in pinning the snake with a broom handle while the dog tore its head off. Billy cursed the father for being away, as the older boy in the story promised his mother he would never go droving.

Billy closed the book and reflected on his own life and his own mother's loneliness and abandonment. He wondered if he was fated to be a drover like his father. Maybe he should go back and comfort his mother. But there was really nothing there for him that he didn't feel he had already outgrown. No, like it or not, his path lay stretched out along the open road. He could only hope that somewhere along the way he would come to grips with what his life was all about. Maybe then he could offer more to a woman than a shack full of kids sequestered away in the bush.

From there his thoughts drifted further and further into his own imagination of the future. He envisioned himself a well-respected, distinguished gentleman living in the city, in Sydney, with a little grey around his temples and a suit of tailored clothes. He would read the paper every morning and stay well educated on world events. Whoever he decided to marry would not have to squat in a dirty shack in the bush. She would be an elegant woman; they would dine out on the town at least once a week and have a nanny to raise the children. He fell asleep with these dreams.

Throughout the remainder of the afternoon, Billy woke from his nap just enough to put another piece of wood on his small fire. He was enjoying every minute of a luxurious siesta—like many a lazy afternoon on the sheep station when he would sneak out back to read in one of his many secret places. Memories came and went as he lay beside the billabong, drifting in and out of a most nourishing dreamtime.

When Doug left the billabong, he jogged up the jungle trail all the way back to town. It wasn't a fast run, just a steady jog. He knew the trail well and enjoyed running it two or three times a week. Once he got close to town, he slowed down to a walk. He liked to keep his composure, and he did not like people to see him sweat.

Walking past the dance theater, he made his way down the street to his mother's thrift store. A few people were loitering in the shop, browsing amongst the secondhand items. "Hi, Mom. How's your day?" he said cheerfully.

Doug's mother smiled when she saw her son. "Mine's great, Doug. How's yours?"

"Good," he said as he walked behind the counter and hugged his mom. "I met a strange boy today. His name is Billy, and he is sixteen years old and homeless."

"Poor dear," said Doug's mother. "He's younger than you are."

"I know. He is a whole year younger than me and already out on the road alone. I took him down to the billabong and told him maybe I would bring him some dinner later on."

"That was very nice of you, dear. But I don't know about tonight. Your father is having some friends over for dinner, and I don't know if there will be any extra. You know how those men can eat."

"Oh no, not more of Dad's friends. They aren't part of the movement are they? Those guys give me the creeps."

"I'm afraid they are, Doug, but they aren't bad. They are good men, and your father is very important to them. He is a brave and serious man."

Doug walked from behind the counter and picked an old military hat off a display rack. His mother's store was a great place for finding clothes for costumes. In a mirror he looked at himself with the hat on. In his imagination he became a buffalo soldier scouting ahead of the cavalry.

"Why does Dad always have to be so serious?" He turned the mirror so he could see his mother over his shoulder. She smiled at him.

"Your father is a busy man, that's all. Try to have patience with him."

"I do. It's just those guys from the movement make me scared. I always feel like something bad is going to happen when they are around."

"Try to have patience with them as well, Doug. They are standing up for the rights of your people."

"I know." Doug turned the mirror away from his mom. For a long minute he stared at himself as a buffalo soldier, then he sighed heavily. "I'll see you at home, Mom. Love ya." Doug threw the hat back on the rack and darted out the door.

Twilight came suddenly, as it is prone to in the tropics, without much of a sunset. One time Billy woke up, and the sky above the trees seemed fairly light. It had to have been only a few minutes later when he opened his eyes and found it completely dark.

A strange sound, like a guttural humming, floated through the air from somewhere on the far side of the billabong. The young man sat up to hear better. The sound was musical in its steady, rolling, wavelike rhythm, rising and falling and bending back on itself in truly uninhibited melodies.

"That must be a dijereedoo," said Billy to the sputtering flames of his dying fire. "But I've never heard it sound so good. Wonder where it's coming from."

With excitement Billy stoked up his fire, adding some larger chunks of wood that he had been saving for later that night. He wanted to build it up to a good blaze so that he could go explore the mysterious music and not come back to a completely extinguished fire. He would just have to find more wood on his return to camp.

A flashlight was something that he hadn't been able to afford, so he usually stuck pretty close to camp after dark. But tonight his curiosity about the music was stronger than his foreboding of dark forests. Doug had said he would stop by an hour or so after dark, but he might get hung up or not show up at all. Besides, Billy didn't really expect to be gone very long. He just wanted to get a look at whoever was playing that dijereedoo so masterfully. He moved his swag a little outside of the ring of light being cast by the fire just in case someone else happened along while he was gone. Everything he owned was in that pack. He definitely couldn't afford to lose it.

Away from the campfire the darkness was nearly complete. Billy made slow progress as he passed the spring and angled down the hill. He thought the going might be a little easier if he stayed closer to the billabong where the ground was flatter and there were less trees and sticks to stumble on and trip over. Hopefully there would be no crocodiles lurking along the banks. With the sound of the gurgling river on his right, he felt confident that he could find his way.

Stopping for a minute beside the river, the young lad listened intently for the magical music of the dijereedoo and to make sure that he was indeed heading toward it. At this point he looked back to see if he could see his camp. But his effort was to no avail. Try as he might, his vision could penetrate the darkness no more than a few yards. He wondered if his fire had already died down, but pushed the notion aside as impossible. The forest was just too dense and the dark night too complete.

When the music stopped, its absence was eerie. The sound of it had become part of the night, and without it there was a definite void. Maybe I should just turn around and go back, he thought. Whoever is playing may not want company, anyway.

But then it started again, this time more haunting than before—like an echo from a very lonely soul. The musician must have just been taking a break to gather his breath and bearing. The imagination and feeling bestowed within the music

19

expressed limitless contemplation and sorrow. Here was a person capable of producing, note for note, the questions and anxieties of his life. The effect was hypnotic. Billy found his feet moving toward the music before he was fully aware of it. He felt like a child or a mouse attracted by the Pied Piper.

His eyes lifted involuntarily toward the heavens, as if looking for guidance. And there he found it. The path was revealed to him. He actually became aware of a difference in light quality directly above the river, as though it cut a shining swath through the encroaching darkness of its tree-lined borders. A star-filled sky could be seen above the river where there were no trees, and, almost like a road map, his eyes could follow the avenue of stars and discern the course to follow. He felt a little ridiculous walking along in the dark forest with his head thrown back and his gaze toward the sky above. He felt a little ridiculous walking along in the dark forest with his head thrown back and his gaze toward the sky above, but somehow he couldn't resist this unorthodox guidance as he plunged headlong into the unknown.

In a very short while he came to the trailhead where he and Doug had first merged with the river. He stood for a moment to judge the direction from which the music came. Satisfied that it was not coming from uphill, he continued on, following the river farther away from the camp. Now he began to wonder if perhaps the music was coming from over the water and whether he would have to find a way across.

How far can this music be travelling? Surely I must be getting close.

The Red Gum trees were growing farther apart, separated by large granite boulders. At first Billy looked for ways around these clumps of rock and trees, but eventually he became boxed in, confronted by a solid rock wall. He stopped and thought again about crossing the river, which was only forty or fifty feet wide at this point.

He reexamined the rock wall and determined that it was really a collection of huge boulders over which he could probably climb. The music had faded away, as though the musician was either taking another break or had quit altogether. Billy stared at the group of boulders.

Then the dijereedoo began its hypnotic rhythm anew. It came from just above him, just beyond the boulders. Billy began to climb. Finding small cracks and contours of the rock to use as steps and handholds, he scrambled up the first, and then the second, in a series of four progressively larger chunks of stone. At the top he could see that he had reached his goal.

In front of him and up one more boulder sat a man with his back toward Billy. He wore a beat-up leather bushman's hat—even though it was dark and he needed no protection from the sun—and blew into a very long, wooden dijereedoo which hung over the side of the boulder. Sitting cross-legged and somewhat hunched over, he seemed completely caught up in the sounds emanating from his slender instrument. Billy settled comfortably on his own rock, waiting, watching, and listening in rapt satisfaction.

The music lifted him far above the tiny rock upon which he sat, far above the entire billabong. Dancing through the jungle treetops, like a thing that knew no bounds, the sound transported him with each delicious note. Without thinking about it analytically or even questioning in any way, Billy understood that what he was hearing was the song of life—the harmonious, never-ending chant of all things. In his mind, he floated and drifted, seeing places, faces, and animals he had never known before. But somehow they were all familiar, as though he himself had indeed been a part of all things for all time.

These thoughts and images came, in a wordless way, to this relatively uneducated young lad, because his mind was open to them. No one had ever expressed to him concepts even vaguely similar to the notions he was now entertaining with ease. He was out of his body, and his timeless soul played freely in a realm attainable by all.

When the music stopped, Billy had a perilous feeling that the entire world hung by a slender thread and that one man, a representative of the human race, stood at the bottom of the thread, where the world was attached, burning the lifeline with a giant disposable lighter. Billy wanted to tackle that man and wrestle away his cataclysmic incinerator before there was no rainforest left and society wilted under a limitless sun. The young lad sitting on the rock felt that if the destructive nature of man wasn't stopped, then the music wouldn't continue, and thus the constant, harmonious, rhythmic roll of the universe would be halted.

"What'sa matta, mate? Ya look like ya've seen a ghost." A happy face—lined, bearded, wrinkled, and brown from the sun—filled Billy's gaze when he came into focus. "And what might you be doin' here?" said he.

"Well, uh, I'm not sure," Billy stumbled, mumbling. "I heard your music."

"So you thought you'd come have a look, eh? Well, that's just fine. Wouldn't mind a bit of company anyway. Come on over to camp; have a bit of tea."

"You really play quite well," Billy managed to articulate, still a little stunned at the sudden turn of events.

"Well? You say I play well? Well, yes, I suppose you're right." The strange man with the friendly smile carried his instrument in his left hand as he climbed down off the rock Billy had sat on. This caused the boy to wonder why he hadn't seen or heard the man climb from the higher rock he had been playing on. But there wasn't time to think about it much; the older man was already out of sight around the next boulder. Billy hurried to catch up.

"So, you're new on the tucker-track, eh? Don't deny it. I can tell. Been on the long road m'self. Hungry? Have you eaten? My name's Leonard, what's yours? Come on, boy, speak up."

Leonard was amazingly spry and agile for his apparently advanced years. He picked his way rapidly through the stones, jumping from rock to rock with very sure feet. In the darkness Billy had a hard time keeping up.

"My name is Billy, and I've been on the track for a spell," he told the man. "How far is your camp? And why were you sitting so far away?"

Just then they came to a cave in the side of the hill. A lantern glowed within.

"Make yourself at home, I have. Should be some hot water on the fire; I'll get the tea."

Billy stayed close to the opening and watched as Leonard busied himself around the cave.

"This is a nice place you've got here. Does anyone else know about it?" inquired the lad.

"Oh, sure. Lots of people know I'm here. Most of the local authorities figure I'm harmless enough, so they let me stay. The acoustics aren't very good though, that's why I like to sit on that rock where you found me. The music carries better from there."

"I should say it does. I heard it quite clearly from the other side of the billabong." Billy was loosening up, gradually becoming more at ease as he glanced around the rough interior. "Did you make those?" he said, indicating the multitude of little wooden carvings perched here and there on rocky ledges and other little niches throughout the cave.

"Yes, those are my creations." Leonard poured hot water from the boiling pan into an earthenware teapot, then set it, with two matching mugs, on a rough-hewn bamboo table beside the fire. There were two bamboo chairs of similar design also beside the fire.

"Please come in and sit down," invited the host. "Welcome to my humble abode."

Billy shook off his lingering apprehension and took a seat by the fire.

"These chairs are really comfortable. I suppose you made them also."

"Could probably say that about most everything in here. Made a go at sellin' these things for a livin' at one point or another in my illustrious career. The plates, mugs, and teapots did pretty well, and the carvings I can sell all day long, as long as I stick with the popular Australian images of koala bears and such. But the bamboo furniture only sold to a few families locally; guess it was too big and bulky for the tourists."

"So, you make your living as an artist," Billy said admiringly.

"More of a craftsman, really. Once in a while I get inspired to create a piece of art." He pointed over his shoulder with his thumb at an elaborate carving, hanging like a painting, on the wall behind him. It depicted an old, bearded aborigine man gazing with consternation at the heavens. The lines on his forehead, and the expression on his face, were etched with such delicate care that it invited the human touch to discern whether or not the onlooker's own imagination had bestowed the life-like interpretation. Billy got up from his seat by the fire to look closer and found that the aborigine man was studying the upper right corner of the carving where closer scrutiny revealed an intricate rendering of the Southern Cross constellation.

"I've never seen anything so beautiful." Billy was awestruck.

"Yeah, once in a while it comes out," Leonard sighed. "But most of the time I think I'm going mad carving endless koalas and kangaroos so that I can buy another bag of beans."

"But this is something to be proud of. To be able to create something like this is a great gift. You're a lucky man. Your life is not meaningless like so many others." Billy returned to his seat by the fire.

"Well, thank you, my young philosopher. Billy, you said your name was, right?"

"Yes, that's right. But I don't remember if I told you or not."

The two new friends sat quiet for a while, watching the flames crackle, thinking about the world and the strange web of interaction that makes up life.

"So, Leonard, what do you know about the Aborigines?" Billy broke the silence. "For some reason I've been thinking about them a lot lately, and I'm not sure why. What is the fascination that we white folk have with their culture?"

Leonard let the question hang for a while, tumbling it around in his brain. It was a question that needed proper contemplation.

"Well, for one thing, they are the oldest culture on earth, and their ways haven't changed since the dawn of time. This gives them an innocence that we have long ago forgotten in our mad rush to evolve. It also puts them more in tune with the natural elements of the world, all of which were written off and condemned as ignorance until recently, when world events dictated a closer understanding of the elemental forces surrounding us all. Now that many people are becoming conscious of the environment, they are looking at how some of the older cultures have achieved harmony with nature, and they are wondering how we can translate that into our own daily lives in a way that would fit into a multitude of different societies. We could all really learn a lot from each other if we try to open our minds to the possibilities.

"I don't remember who said it, maybe I read it in a *National Geographic*, but somewhere I recently read a profound quote. It simply said, 'We must look to the past to find a pathway into the future.' I believe that to be a truism."

Billy shifted in his chair and sat up a little straighter. He felt so intellectual, sitting with this man of the world, having such a highly conceptual conversation. He held on to the arm of the chair for balance and stability.

Doug slouched at the dinner table with his mother, his father and two other men. The two other men and his father did most of the talking in broken English and an aborigine dialect different from the Tjapukai. One of the men didn't seem to understand the English when it was used, and he relied upon his friend to convey what little he had to say. Doug said hardly a word as he toyed with his mashed potatoes and salad, pushing aside the fried chicken.

"But, Jim," Rebecca interrupted the men's conversation, "why did they have to break the windows? Couldn't they have just opened them?"

Doug's father turned to look at his wife. "I thought you understood these things, Rebecca. You always have in the past. It was passion. It just isn't natural for these people to live in boxes."

"I understand that," she said. "But I don't understand why they always have to break things. And then to go so far as to start a fire in the living room as though it were a cave. I just think it is too much. Where is the respect for the land that you are always talking about?"

Jim looked momentarily at the other two men sitting quietly humbled, then he refocused. "Respect for the land does not reside in those government houses. They are an insult to people with a heritage of wandering."

Doug wished he could leave the table.

"It was a mistake, Rebecca," Jim continued. "They didn't expect to burn down the building."

"What? They burned a building?" Doug sat up in his chair.

"Yes, they did." Jim looked at Doug paternally. "Actually six houses burned down before the fire department could get there and put the blaze out."

"Oh, my God," said Doug's mother. "Was anybody hurt?"

"No, everybody got out of the houses." Jim looked briefly at the other two men. "It was a party that got out of hand. But it was inevitable. There is a lot of frustration on the reservations and a very deep desire to return to the old ways. They wanted to dance naked around a fire in a cave, but they have no caves, so they blew hand paintings on the walls of one of the houses, broke out all of the windows, and started a small fire. Then, of course, it got out of control. They would have let every house there burn if the fire department hadn't come along to stop it."

"We are sorry now," the man who knew English said from the end of the table.

Feelings of anxiety began to build in Doug's stomach.

"Oh, Jim," Doug's mother said with worry, "these men are going to be wanted for arson. They can't be here. I'm surprised the police haven't been here already to talk to you about them. Things are getting so dangerous for us already."

"What kind of danger?" Doug said with concern.

"Now just calm down, Rebecca. We haven't done anything wrong." Jim was starting to lose his patience.

Rebecca stood up from the table and began scooping food onto an extra plate. "Doug, maybe you should go see if your new friend is hungry."

The boy was grateful that his mother was looking out for him. "Thanks, Mom," he said.

Right then a knock was heard at the front door. The two fugitives got up from the table in a frightened rush.

"Please answer the door, Doug," said his father. "And you two men sit down."

Doug went nervously to the door and opened it to see three familiar policemen from town and one man, without a uniform, that he did not recognize.

"Good evening, Doug," said Officer Hardy. "I'd like to speak with your dad, if that's okay."

The fourth man, wearing a trenchcoat, pushed forward. "This is official business, not a pleasant visit. We have a warrant to search this house for two fugitives wanted on federal charges. Now, move aside, boy." He pushed Doug out of the way and entered the house.

"What is the meaning of this?" Jim got up from the table as the man entered the room.

Seeing the other two men at the table, the federal agent drew a pistol from under his trenchcoat.

"Nobody move!" He waved the gun from person to person. "Everyone here is under arrest!"

The three local police drew their guns in support of that statement.

"So, what you're saying is that mankind has evolved far enough and that, if we don't stop now, we're going to destroy the world?" Billy felt like a wizard to have put those ideas together.

"No, my young friend, that is not what I meant to say. Quite the contrary really, although I can well imagine how you could hear that in my words. No, what I really meant to convey is that I believe we all need to make one more giant step on the evolutionary ladder. By embracing our past, learning from one another, and bridging the gaps between our various cultures, we can create a more universal society that is in a more harmonious balance with nature and that draws on the diversity of the world for the benefit of all. Plants, animals, water, soil, machinery, knowledge, and hardship, it's all interrelated." Leonard's eyes had a wonderful sparkle when he became animated in conversation. It had been quite a while since he had any company with whom to share his thoughts.

"Now, I hope I didn't scare you off or confuse you by lettin' loose with all my cannons at once. I just got so many things to say but have never been blessed with the ability to put them in proper order. Say it all at once, direct as possible, that's my style."

"Well, I suppose it's better'n havin' nothin' to say," said Billy. "Lots o' times I just can't think of anything except what someone else is sayin'."

"But you're doin' fine now, aren't you? No worries about what to say now, right? You seem like a levelheaded lad," Leonard pulled on his own knees to lever himself out of his chair. "You remind me a bit of myself at your age. Boy, did I take the world serious. Not only did I know everything, but I also thought that all the problems of the world were mine alone to bear. Please stop me if I bore you. I seldom have company without a purpose. Every visitor takes something away, even if only a story." The wizened man moved a short ways away from the fire, seeming to gather strength from his familiar surroundings. He turned to face Billy, who sat watching him as though he were intellect incarnate.

"You followed my music here because your wondering, wandering soul is seeking answers to the timeless questions of generations. You have come to me to glean what I have learned and thus make your own road a little easier. That is good; it is in the natural order of things.

"So, listen for a while, make yourself comfortable, and I will tell you of the time when I was a seeker of answers, like yourself."

Leonard seemed to stand a little more erect, ran both hands down his chest to smooth his shabby clothing, then turned slightly away from Billy and began his tale.

"For most of my childhood I was a somber lad, spent much of my time brooding over silly little things that now I wouldn't consider worth the digression. I was hardly ever cheerful. Of course, no one in our run-down neighborhood of Belfast was very cheerful in those days. Most of Northern Ireland was in hard times when I was a kid. At least that's how I remember it. The religious bickering and petty wars between the Protestants and the Catholics always got in the way of any fun.

"Then there was my father. He was so caught up in it all that he really didn't pay much attention to me, especially when I didn't show any enthusiasm for his cause. My little sister was the opposite of me. She became so righteously involved in all the church programs that she was quickly sequestered away into the inner sanctum of their realm of knowledge.

"That was all right by me. As long as they focused their attention on her, it left me free to escape their cloistered walls and rove about the country a bit. I would have been quite happy, except that my thoughts invariably turned to brooding. In the little bit of time my father spared for me, he was able to fully convince me that I was an evil child, a lazy loafer whose delinquent ways would surely lead down the long road to purgatory.

"So, I became a bit of an outcast, from the family anyway." Leonard paced around the room as he spoke, picking up small carvings from time to time, turning them over in his hands absentmindedly as he followed the thread of his narration.

"Fate is a funny thing," he said, returning from his reverie. "For a seeker of answers to be banished to a land where questions are seldom asked seems cruel, and yet it is the perfect solution. I thought my father's final admonishments had come true that last Sunday when I skipped the church service and wandered the hills feeling lowly and despicable. I had no idea that my misguided youthful deviations would save my life. How could I have known that an angry member of the opposing religion would heave a pipe-bomb through the stained-glass window of our local cathedral? And no one could have predicted that the homemade device would roll down the aisle with the grotesque purpose of annihilating the preacher, my front row family, and all but two of the choir boys.

"It seems like an outlandish nightmare or a chapter in some uncivilized history to imagine the chain of events that took place in so short a time. The religious factions of Belfast erupted in a full scale Holy War that killed and wounded hundreds of people. I thought it was all my fault because I hadn't gone to church, so I walked around in a daze mumbling, 'What have I done?' until finally my relatives sent me away to the promised land down under. They said I was lucky to be leaving the old country, to have a chance at something new. I thought I had stumbled on my father's legendary road to hell."

"My father had his own road to hell," Billy mumbled without elaboration.

"There are many different trails leading into that pit, I'm sure. But the one I found myself on was a dry, dusty track out back of Broken Hill, down in southern New South Wales. Of course, my tormented fifteen-year-old psyche was quick to rename it Broken Hell, which, in turn, caused me to be able to see nothing nice about the place. I was pretty much convinced that the condition of the world, as I knew it, was directly connected to my daydreaming and brooding. It didn't take much of an intellectual leap for my anguished mind to decide that humanity might be a lot better off without me in the picture.

"But, I couldn't just kill myself. Not after all my other blasphemies. I knew I'd end up in the Big Pit for sure if I took my life with my own hands.

"So then the method of my demise became a logistics problem that occupied and entertained my mind for the first several weeks that I was in Australia. I concocted all kinds of various schemes that would place the actual means of my departure in the hands of an innocent. I dreamed of stepping in front of a speeding train or being eaten by a killer shark while diving for shellfish. But Broken Hell was too far away from the coast, and I might have had to swim around for a long time waiting for a shark to get me.

"My poor, tormented soul spent a lot of time with this dilemma, weighing the pros and cons of just about every conceivable way that a lad might die. And, in the meantime, I was getting to know and actually be quite fond of my aunt Anna, whom I'd been sent to stay with. She was, at that time, a feisty, ambitious, single woman in her early twenties, with curly red hair, clear and sincere blue eyes, and a spirit that couldn't be broken. But what I found most attractive about her was that she didn't go to church. She believed in God, she told me, but she didn't believe that God was to be found inside stone walls and stained glass.

"She was way ahead of her time, and brave enough to believe her own thoughts. She insisted that a Godlike presence was within us and even in the smallest, most insignificant things, like a rock. I found this concept very hard to grasp at first, after the mental pounding that my father had dished out. But, the more I listened to her, the more I realized that she spoke the truth, and what a beautiful truth it was." Leonard stood quiet for a moment, lost again inside a memory.

"I was such a confused young lad. Right at the time when I should have been discovering my own manhood and chasing young girls, I began to fall inescapably in love with my own aunt. She was the most beautiful, vibrant, and enlightened woman I'd ever imagined. I dreamed forlornly of a life spent with her at my side. The world would have been ours, to do with as we pleased, if only we weren't related."

"Was she your father's sister or your mother's?" Billy interrupted, wanting to get the story right.

"Oh, I'm sorry. I guess I didn't make that clear," Leonard apologized. "She was actually the illegitimate child of my mother's father, who moved to Australia after a much-publicized scandal involving him with the wife of a prominent Irish diplomat. Anna was much younger than my mother and was only in contact with the rest of my family through the complete insistence of my grandfather. He denied the existence of God and maintained the notion that heaven was to be found here on earth, preferably in the arms of multiple women. But then again, he was killed by a jealous husband before Anna was ten years old." Leonard paused once again in his narration.

"I realize that I have digressed several times from my original topic. But, if you hear me out, I will eventually bring this around so that it relates to you and your question about the Aborigines. I have to bring it around this way or else you might not understand it completely. You see, it was because of my disturbed childhood and my unfulfilled love for Anna that I came to know and understand the mysterious ways of the Aborigine."

"How's that?" Billy shifted again in his chair and drank the last of his tea. "You wouldn't have any tobacco would you?"

"Actually, I do. I keep it around for the occasional visitor. Gave it up years ago myself, but I understand the desire." The aged storyteller moved to the back of his cave and rummaged around in a cardboard box. "Here it is. I hope it's not too stale." He handed the young man a pouch, half-filled with fine tobacco, and some rolling papers.

"That's great! Thank you very much. I'll only use a little, and please go on with your story; it's got my interest." Billy scooted to the front edge of his chair and held the bag between his knees while he rolled himself a smoke.

"Use as much as you like; I can always get more. Truly all things are provided." Leonard enjoyed seeing his guest happy. "But, back to Anna. She talked a lot about the darkfellows back then, with the utmost respect, which was not a popular view at the time. She believed in their concept of dreamtime, which was then only partially understood by local scholars, and she greatly respected their ability to live in harmony with the harsh conditions that surrounded them. How she came to possess this knowledge was a mystery to me. She prophesied that their way of life would be instrumental in studies that would bring about the saving grace of the world.

"I've had many a year to think about the things she told me as a lad, and I know now that every word she spoke was as true as any gospel religion. It's been more than forty years, and now the rest of the world is just starting to take notice."

"But tell me how you came to understand all of this and how it related to your life." Billy had finished rolling his cigarette and now lit it with a stick he had poked into the fire. He blew out the first papery puff and then inhaled deeply, holding the smoke in his lungs with obvious satisfaction.

"I was just gettin' to that. You see, it wasn't until I left Broken Hill that some of what Anna was sayin' started to make sense. She had always been talkin' about balance and harmony an' doin' without so that others might have a little later on; about lookin' to the future an' not usin' up everything we have; and, somehow, these were just not notions that I was real comfortable with. I was still havin' a hard time tryin' to realize that the inevitable doom of the world was not entirely my burden to bear. I pretty much still clung to the idea that it was only through my demise that the sins of at least my family would be absolved." Leonard shrugged and sighed, rubbing the inner corners of both eyes with his right thumb and index finger.

"As I said before," he continued, "I was a mixed up boy." He waved away the thought with a backstroke of the same hand. "So, I set off for the outback, determined to perish, not from my own hand, but from the elements. I simply would not eat or drink anything and therefore would eventually just sort of drop dead.

"But I couldn't let my beloved aunt Anna know of my outcome; it would surely upset her to know that I had thrown away my own life when there was so much opportunity ahead for me. I made up my mind that I would have to put some distance between Broken Hill and the spot where I finally fell over into my own little broken hell.

"I didn't have much money, but I had earned a little doing odd jobs for some of the parents Anna knew through school. She wouldn't have me just hangin' around her place in the afternoons and had gotten those jobs for me to fill my idle hours.

"Anyway, I looked at a few maps and decided that the Plains of Nullarbor looked desolate and deserted enough to get lost in. So I bought a ticket on the railway going west to Perth and figured I'd ride the train until we stopped at a small station somewhere in the middle of the plains, and then I'd simply walk off into the sunset. I was sixteen then. Anna knew I was looking for a way out. I told her I was going to find work in the diamond mines of Western Oz. She knew it was a lie, but she didn't try to stop me."

"How long had you been in Australia?"

"Only about six months."

"And you still believed so strongly that the death of your family was your fault?"

"Yes. Somehow I just couldn't let go of it. It's not an easy thing to get over."

"But, to kill yourself, that's pretty serious."

"I was an idealist. Besides, I knew I should never love Anna. I was young—a young, romantic idealist." The elder orator looked across the room at the juvenile inquisitor. "Please be patient; the part you've been waiting for is coming up. I want to tell you how the Aborigines changed my life. Have you heard of the Pintupi? They are a tribe of no-madic wanderers that you might find outback of Kalgoorlie. But I shouldn't get ahead of myself.

"I took the train as far as Ooldea, and the whole way there I ate as much as possible. There was a good dining car on the train, which I took full advantage of, and several of the stations we stopped at had cheap restaurants. I had made my mind up that I would carry no food or water on my little walkabout, but I didn't want to die on the edge of some town and have someone find my body. Therefore I figured I'd better eat well so I'd make it a respectable distance away.

"And it was also for this reason of wanting to put a few miles behind me that I couldn't quite decide whether or not to carry just a little water. For sure I would carry no food, but I had always liked water, and the thought of getting out in the middle of that dry desolation without even a sip of water made me just about lose my nerve for the whole venture.

"In the end, what good sense I did have won out, so that when I got off the train in the hot afternoon and stood on the weather-beaten wooden platform that served as a station for Ooldea, I had nothing but the clothes I wore, with a little money in the pockets, and a canteen of water I had bought along the way.

"I walked to one side and waited, trying to look nonchalant, as two darkfellows loaded a flatbed wagon with dried goods. One of them had gotten off the train with me and was met there by the other man and a much older-looking fellow who didn't leave the wagon. He just sat there, with his white hair and his dark skin, seeming to be asleep beneath a wide-brim hat, while holding the reins of a lazy donkey whose one desire was shade. I empathized with the animal while trying to remain uninterested.

"When the dust cleared after the train pulled away, I turned to see three Aborigines seated across the bench of the wagon. Their backs were toward me as they started off down the track with the old man in the middle, still in control of the reins, though the donkey certainly needed no guidance. There wasn't another road—just the one dusty track as far as I could see. I watched them and wondered if they would be the last living humans I would see. Then suddenly, the old man in the middle turned his head almost a hundred an' eighty degrees to look at me. His body barely moved. He stared at me, and I shivered as his wrinkled mouth gaped in a wide toothless grin." Leonard paused a moment for effect.

"I can still see that face clearly. I wonder what secret merriment he delighted in.

"But, anyway, on with the story. I waited a good long while for that wagon to get completely out of sight down that long, straight dirt road. Like I said, it was the only road around, and it led into Ooldea or Waralinga, I supposed, or maybe to a crossroads. Somewhere, I didn't care. I proposed never to follow another road again. It was the trackless unknown for me as long as I lasted, which could be at least forty-eight hours, I reasoned. Or maybe several days, if I rationed my water. The idea of dying had a sort of ebb and flow in its attraction.

"When the wagon was long gone, I still loitered around the ramshackle station. I guess I was reluctant to leave that last vestige of the world I had known. But finally, with that old man's queer look still on my mind, I stepped across the tracks and never looked back.

"If I was lacking in some facets of my character, it certainly wasn't in my willingness to commit to something. Some folks can get all wishy-washy and change their minds on things time an' again. But not me, no mate, not back then. I'd get an idea in my head an' hang on to it. I had become determined to walk until I fell over dead, and that was what I set out to do.

"Now, being in this narrow state of mind, I was not prone to noticing a whole lot more than what was right in front of me, which precluded my seeing the grand abandonment I was walking into. It was probably better that I didn't see the whole picture, or I might not have made it as far as I did. But I wonder, when I think of it, if there wasn't someone else watching, someone who did notice the way the evening came on slowly and turned the sky pink.

"For me, it was seemingly endless sand dunes. I was making my way north as best as I could, hoping to get into a small group of hills barely visible on the horizon. I figured that maybe there I could find a shady spot behind some rock where I

could lie down comfortably for my final rest—
somewhere that my body might not be found for a
little while. I didn't figure I'd make it till the next
day, so I just walked until it got dark and then laid
down in the sand. I drank from my canteen and
watched the Southern Cross rise to the left of a half
moon.

"Next day I was under way by dawn. I had
slept well, pitched out under the stars with no
blankets or frills. I wasn't hungry until late morning after I'd been walking for several hours. The
morning had been cool, and the walking had been
stimulating. I marveled at how well I felt. But by
noon it had gotten hot, and my energy level had
dropped considerably. I sweated profusely and
wished I had a wide-brim hat like the one the
white-haired gentleman with the meaningful
smile wore. I began to get unreasonably nervous
and looked back over my shoulder frequently as
though someone might be following me. Trying to
control my wandering mind was almost an effort
equal to that of my physical being in its endless
march. I thought of Anna and her glorious intellect. I thought of my father and his ceaseless admonishments, and I thought of myself and my own
dogged determination for extinction.

"It was that final bit of self-examination that
turned my life around. It was as though I had to go
through this whole melodramatic act all the way to
this point of deprivation to finally catch a glimpse
of self-worth. Slowly, beyond each new dune that
passed under my feet, I began to see a new horizon

as my consciousness rose out of my body and revealed to me my physical insignificance. I could see myself as though through a bird's eyes, and the land around me was mapped out for miles. I saw how burdened my physical being appeared as it plodded its way across the trackless dunes. But burdened by what? I carried nothing but a small, cheap canteen. It was my own conscience that burdened me so. It distressed me greatly to think that I had saddled myself with such an irrelevant load. I had to look away from that poor struggling beast that I knew as myself, so I looked forward to the hills.

"It became obvious to me that my body's endurance would last only through the day, but hopefully, by nightfall, I would be safely ensconced in some niche in those hills.

"For the rest of the day, as my body plodded forward, I took advantage of my lofty point of view. Nothing much was happening on the Plains of Nullarbor that day. A few grey and black vultures circled high above, waiting for me to fall over and end my plight. A small oasis of Coolibah and gum trees promised shade and security behind some distant dunes to the east. The tracks of some unseen animals crisscrossed and obscured my prints from the day before, and through the middle of the vast loneliness ran—straight as a line on graph paper—the seemingly endless railroad.

"By the end of the day I was completely thrashed and wasted from my trek. I had rationed my water so that I still had a few mouthfuls when I reached the first rocky swells of the hills. Drawing on my last reserve of strength, I scaled a stony precipice to a point that I believed to be a peak. But, upon achieving that ambitious perch, I could see that the hills stretched out for miles and that I had barely penetrated their density. I sat down where I stood and felt the vastness of my whole universe crowd into a pinpoint on that one rocky ledge. The sun began to set, and in its absence the cold air of night swirled around to remind me how alone and ill-prepared I was. The sweat of my day's exertions gave way to goose bumps that covered my skin and caused me to shake with chill.

"Now, I know it may seem like I'm taking my time bringing this story around to its point, but the truth is that if a story isn't told in its entirety, then the storyteller is doing the listener an injustice by not allowing him to equip his imagination with all the possible details. Besides, the night is still young, and you came to me to hear this story even if you didn't realize it. Would you care for more tea?"

"No, I'm fine, and please don't worry, I'm followin' the story real well."

"Well, that makes me happy. It has been a while since I've had an appreciative audience. Think I'll make myself another cup."

Leonard walked to the back of the cave and filled the teapot with water from a large wooden barrel.

"So, you're sittin' out on this ledge an' you're shiverin'," Billy restarted the old man's tale. "Why didn't you build a fire?"

"I might have, if I could have. But I didn't have any matches to start one, and there really wasn't any wood around to burn; none that I could see, anyway. But that is an example of how green I was. If I had more sense or knowledge of nature, I'd have seen that the cliffs around me were made of flint, and there was plenty of sagebrush that I could have burned. But those are things I didn't know until Ben Ben found me."

"Ben Ben?" Billy looked quizzically at Leonard as he leaned forward to put the pot on to boil.

"Yes, Ben Ben was my savior. He came to me after I sat on the rock for two days. I had found a cleft in the rock close to the ledge, and there I huddled and shivered the first night away.

"In the morning I rolled out onto the ledge again, to lie in the sunshine and warm my body like a lizard. For some reason I still couldn't get up enough gumption to save myself by returning to civilization. Maybe it was just too much energy and didn't seem worth it on that hot day.

"Anyway, I just laid around all day, dreaming mostly—of the green, rolling hills of Ireland. By the time the sun began to set again, I was barely conscious, spread out on my ledge completely absorbed in the brilliant display of colors.

"When darkness finally set in, my dreams had turned to nightmares of hell and punishment. I shook sometimes, involuntarily, and not entirely from the cold; it was my dreams causing me to flail about. Doom, darkness, and eternal suffering—isn't it amazing how the mind can be programmed?

I was filled with so much fear that I was trying to reconcile. Suffice it to say that I spent a truly dreadful night atop that hill.

"But then dawn came, and Ben Ben was there building a fire and cooking small cakes on hot rocks. He was young, thin but muscular, very flat-black and wearing only a pair of faded denim shorts. He flipped the cakes nimbly with his fingers and smiled at me when he said, 'G'day, mate.'

"'Same to ya, mate,' I said. 'Where'd you come from?'

"'Down a ways,' he replied.

"I sat up wearily and rubbed my eyes blearily. 'What ever that is you're cookin', it sure smells good,' I told him.

"'Good, good, you share, like a lot.' He smiled again.

"When he had four hot cakes cooked, he handed two of them to me. We ate in silence except when I told him how good I thought his cakes were. He showed me a small, canvas backpack in which he carried a small amount of supplies.

"We talked a little after the meal, and he told me his name was Ben Ben because his father was named Ben, and so it was natural that he should be called Ben Ben.

"Ben Ben told me that he was from the Pintupi tribe from the Great Western Desert and that he was out on a walkabout following the songline of the Kookaburra, which was his totem or Dreaming. He was born in the time of the Kookaburra Dreaming, so his dream was the creation song of that laughing, happy bird. Ben Ben was, in turn, a very happy lad and prone to smiling frequently. He was happy simply because his Dreaming was that of the popular, far-ranging prankster of the outback, whose bird call was so preposterous that it could only be heard in this land of oddities.

"Ben Ben enjoyed having the Kookaburra as his totem, for it presented him with a very long songline that could take him completely around the country if he chose to follow it. Not that every Aborigine follows his or her songline from beginning to end. A lot of them didn't bother with it anymore. They were moving into towns and learning the white man's ways. But not the Pintupi. They were one of the last tribes to wander freely without governmental intervention. Ben Ben's father, Ben, had been of the Emu Dreaming and was a leader of their tribe."

"Wait a minute," Billy interrupted. "Now, Ben Ben was of the Kookaburra Dreaming, but his father was of the Emu Dreaming, and yet they were obviously part of the same tribe. How is that?"

"Simple. Your Dreaming is a personal thing that has to do mainly with the place and time you were born. It really has nothing to do with the rest of the tribe. Kind of like the Zodiac signs of Astrology that the Greeks conceived of, only there are a lot more possibilities in the Aboriginal dreamtime myth.

"To put the whole thing in a simple picture, imagine that, at the dawn of time more than fifty thousand years ago, all the characters of Aboriginal mythology walked upon the land in a dreamlike vision, all singing a song of creation. Occasionally they would cross paths with each other, and thereby they would name one another and incorporate that name into their song of creation. They also named plants, trees, and other things they saw. These became major landmarks for all time. The Aborigines believe that all of reality is more or less an hallucination, and that nothing really exists in a physical sense until it is sung into being. That is essentially what the songlines are all about. They are a way of telling the original experiences of the Emu or Kookaburra or the Platypus or Koala Bear. Everything has a song, and by following the songline a person is better able to understand his or her totem." The old man paced around while he waited for the water to boil in the teapot.

"Have you ever heard the concept that all the universe was originally music sung by a chorus of the gods? Many religions are rooted in this idea of an ever-expanding tapestry of harmonious melodies. It wasn't until Lucifer sang a little out of key, trying to show off by doing something different, that a discordance was noticed, and the distinction between good and bad became apparent.

"From that point on, the universe began to solidify and the planets to take shape, with one spinning one way and another spinning another way. Gravity developed as a natural boundary, and matter became a heavy thing. No longer was everything one and the same as it was in the beginning. Proportion, size, and shape became factors, and from that point our whole bumbling world began its chaotic evolution. Do you see how closely that intertwines with the mythology of Dreamtime? Nothing is real until it is perceived."

"I was with you for most of that," Billy said, sitting up straighter and trying to collect his thoughts. "But what happened to you and Ben Ben? Maybe we should stick a little closer to earth. I'm just a poor country boy, you know. Most of that stuff is kinda over my head."

"I'm sorry if I confused you" Leonard apologized. "Sometimes I can get pretty excited."

"That's okay. You've probably had a lot of time to think about all this, and the way you put it, it does make a lot of sense. But what about Ben Ben? Did you guys travel together after that? I can tell you didn't stay on the rock to die."

"Yeah, good ol' Ben Ben—he was quite a mate—became my mentor or spiritual guide for more than twenty years. Taught me stuff I never would have learned on my own. You see, he was on sort of a vision quest, to fully realize the extent of his totem, the Kookaburra—although sometimes I thought he was just out for a long walkabout and was using his vision quest to see the country and for an excuse not to go home. But, that's what it's really all about anyway—to experience the land and live with open eyes and an open mind.

"It can be very hard to put all this into English terms. In a sense, Ben Ben was closer to realizing a Godlike state of mind than anyone I've ever had the pleasure of meeting. He was such a joy to be

51

around, constantly intrigued by even the smallest things, yet with an overall understanding that was limitless in its capacity. He added new concepts to the traditional ones, as though he was the actual Kookaburra dreaming them into existence. Nothing was so sacred that it couldn't stand a little innovation. I guess that was part of his totem—the ability to laugh in the face of authority. Not that he didn't respect convention—he revered the old, oral traditions quite highly. They were his link, his very reason for being. But he could also see that adaptation was part of the same evolutionary chain.

"So, anyway, the reason he came into my life was because of that old man with the funny smile and the buggy, back at the train station. Ben Ben had been travelling for over a month, following the songline that had been sung to him by his tribe. You see, there is a whole other dimension to the songlines that I suppose I'd better explain. If a songline is very long, like that of the Kookaburra, spanning a large area or even the whole continent, then it is often broken into smaller songs, each pertaining to a special region or landmark, and each relating the life-giving sustenance that might be found in that area—like water, for example, and hunting grounds for indigenous plants and animals. All major songlines are more or less links between water holes, and, by learning each of the smaller parts to the song, you can, by following the directions within the song, make your way through some of the harshest environments on earth."

"But, wait a minute," Billy was quite interested. This was some valuable information, and it was coming together in a way that he was able to visualize. "How do you learn all the smaller parts if all you have is the vague idea of the whole song?" This was a vital question to Billy. He felt like he was about to win the jackpot and that bells and alarms would surely go off as soon as he learned the answer to that one question.

"Quite simply," said Leonard with another whimsical wave of his hand. "You learn it from the people that you meet along the way. Like that old man at the station, he was a keeper of verse. In his small part of the world, that man knew the verses to every songline that passed that way. He was a tribal elder. Ben Ben had heard of him from another tribe at a waterhole outside of Rawlinna, and he was on his way to see the man at the station but instead had met the man on the road. The old man knew Ben Ben was coming to see him; he had heard of his walkabout through the voices that come to him on the wind."

"Hold on, mate. What's this about voices that come to him on the wind? You're not tryin' to feed me some kind of hocus-pocus, are you?" Billy was almost offended.

"No, lad, I wouldn't do that to ya. This is the truth as I know it. There is so much I could tell you about the Aborigines, I'm just not sure how far to go. I could tell you what a wonderful and gifted people they are, and how divinely in tune with the

53

world they are, but that has almost become an exception. You could easily find a hundred cases that prove me wrong. By saying, 'voices in the wind,' what I'm really talking about is completely nonverbal, telepathic communication at the highest level attained by mortals on earth. Some of the most evolved Aborigines are capable of sending and receiving telepathic messages for many miles. I've never known if there is a limit to how far they can be separated, but I know it takes a completely open mind—harboring no secrets or doubts—and that there are usually two or three members of a tribe who are capable of it. Sometimes the whole tribe can participate on a local level, but usually these are very nomadic tribes who have had very little influence from white society. I've been trying a form of this communication with my dijereedoo, trying to locate Ben Ben. I'm not sure where he is, but if I play with a completely open mind, then maybe he will hear it." Leonard looked at Billy to see if the boy had followed him.

"That's great," Billy said thoughtfully, "no worries, if you can do it."

Leonard smiled and returned to his story. "But, anyway, the man with the white hair and foolish grin was a very kind and thoughtful man. He told Ben Ben not only the verses of song that he needed to know, but also told him of a white boy who wandered into the desert but must not die. He said that in the course of Ben Ben's experience, he would find me and keep me with him, until my eyes were open and I could see clearly.

"Of course that took the better part of twenty years, but what an awakening! I could not have gotten a better education at any university in the world. I was completely transformed.

"Really, it was a learning experience for both of us. Ben Ben had only had very limited exposure to white culture. His tribal elders had sheltered him as best they could. He had been chosen early on to be a special one, and the elders had placed great gifts of heritage before him so that he might choose the enlightened path. You see, in their culture it is completely up to the individual to decide their own life course. Ben Ben might have wanted to be a toolmaker or an artist or even a town drunkard; it was completely up to him. As it was, he chose the path of enlightenment, much to the pleasure of the elders, who heaped upon him all the knowledge they could.

"Then they suggested the walkabout so that he could learn from other tribes and maybe even the white man, and then come back to them as a wiser man than any who had previously led their clan. They could see that the world was becoming an increasingly complicated place, so they had great hope that Ben Ben would see his way through, and be able to rise above the intricacies, then come back to lead his people on a path that would allow them to endure the troublesome years to come. They knew it was a gamble and that it would take a long time for Ben Ben to complete his journey, if he completed it at all, but they could see the need for it, and so it came to be.

"But that first morning that we were together," Leonard let go of one narrative to return to the original, "we had to backtrack a little to get back on the course he was following. I had no idea where we were going, or why I was even following him. But it did seem like a better thing to do than to sit on that dumb rock waiting to die. Besides, my new friend, this young darkfellow, was most insistent that I come with him.

"We climbed back down from the rocks and traced our way back into the middle of the sand dunes, to a point completely vast and bereft of points of reference, and it was here that Ben Ben—who I thought had been muttering to himself or chanting something the whole way—decided to stop and begin a sort of dance in a circle that stopped at four distinct spots in the sand. For fifteen minutes he did this, and then he started marching off across the dunes.

"That fifteen minutes of ritual dance was something Ben Ben did each time we set off on our journey. He wouldn't do it if we were loitering in some town or working for a rancher somewhere, which we did a lot, but when we were back on the songline, he'd start each march with this circle dance. I learned from my many years of association with him that he was drawing all the spirits together to ask for safe passage, and to request that any of the plant or animal species that were nearby to reveal themselves so that we could find nourishment from their embodiment.

56

"I learned that through the years the various other forms of life had volunteered to help feed the displaced aboriginal humans when the white settlers came and forced them from their abundant coastal habitat to the harsh, inhospitable outback. It was because of this agreement that Ben Ben felt no worries about starvation. It was just inevitable that some type of nourishment would present itself. I could describe delicacies I shared with him in places where I would have died alone—things that would bend your mind in an upheaval of disgust, but would also delight you in the right circumstance. Grubs, worms, larvae, things like that.

"Another thing I learned was the importance of following the songlines exactly. They are timed so that to miss a single phrase or sentence or word would, by that degree of omission, cause disorientation. But, if you followed the song exactly, you would be bountifully rewarded by finding patches of dried weeds that might have a tuber or potato-like thing growing beneath the sand. Or, at another spot in the song, you might be told to poke a long reed—which hopefully you picked when you passed them a day or two back in the song, at a time when you had no use for them—into the vast expanse of sand and to suck out water. That's right, water out of a reed poked into the sand.

"Apparently, when the first Kookaburra ventured through those parts, there was a marvelous fountain of water that was promptly recorded in the rhythm of the song. The water is still there, only it is underground. The reeds were always used for sipping the water and are used today for the same purpose, only now they must be poked two or three feet into the sand."

Billy sat staring at Leonard, his mouth slightly agape. Could this old man be mad? Gone a bit looney from living in the cave too long? He never had been very emotionally stable, from what Billy had gathered. Maybe it was time to find an excuse to leave.

"There's really no need to. I won't harm you." Leonard stared back at Billy. "No need to leave, I mean. I know that you were thinking about it— little trick I learned from Ben Ben. Unconscious thought really screams to be heard. It is quite deafening once you're attuned to it. Too bad it has always been a major stumbling block for most cultures. But, as you can see, I learned a little bit about it from my aboriginal friends. It is really quite simple once you remember that your mind is fluid; let it flow. Thoughts are liquid—the fabled stream of consciousness. If you hear that stream murmuring somewhere deep inside you, babbling its secrets among the pebbles on the shore, then follow it, lad. For in the music of those waters you will find your natural rhythm.

"Imagine your mind is a billabong, a mental wellspring, if you will, issuing forth concepts and ideas. It is all fluid and flows through you and from you. It fuels your imagination and arouses your curiosity. In your dreams you see it most clearly and wonder at the disjointed complexity when you awaken.

"That is but an example. Imagine your mind so completely open that all thought flowed through it on a conscious level!! It happens for me when I carve on wood. I hold the wood loosely and observe it a while, then my hands begin to release the image as it flows to me from the wood.

"Also with the dijereedoo, I can play in the waters of abandonment. The heavens open up for me when I play that simple instrument. The resonance reverberates the rhythm of my soul, and I can swim effortlessly through the currents of the universe. The sound of sounds invites me to the wellspring of consciousness, with a pull as insistent as the tides.

"It calls to you, too, I'm sure. In your dreams you are tantalized with the first inklings of the reality you really want to live within. It is all completely up to you to create. There is nothing in this world that is unattainable to you. But always remember the balance. Harmony is a delicate thing.

"I must watch myself not to tell you too much. Already you doubt what I say, and yet it was you who sought me out. You heard the music, and it brought you here so that you could hear the wisdom I have learned, so that it might help you on your own road.

"Right now you are a self-educated, contemplative, young lad, and it is my extreme pleasure to encourage in you the virtues of an open mind. I have a feeling of completion in having related to you the importance of that one, single thing—keeping an open mind."

Without any warning, and almost as though it were audio punctuation for Leonard's last statement, lightning brightened the opening of the cave with its eerie, blue-white luminescence. Thunder rolled across the heavens, and the rain began immediately. Billy got up and walked over to the doorway, looking outside anxiously. Leonard joined him, and the two stood side by side, entranced by the downpour.

"Just a squall," said Leonard. "Should play itself out pretty quick. The earth is cleansing itself."

"What time d'you s'pose it is?" Billy asked.

"Couldn't tell you exactly, must be past midnight though. Have you got a date?"

Billy turned to look at the old man whose eyes squinted in a grin.

"As a matter of fact," said the youth, "I had told a guy named Doug that he might find me camped down here."

"Do you mean Doug, the dancer?"

"Yeah. Why? Do you know him?"

"Oh, yes. He brings me most of my visitors, and his mother runs the thrift store in town. She is a wonderful, kindhearted woman that introduced me to several gallery owners in Sydney. She's white, you know, comes from the city. Studied Aborigines in the university and then came up here to settle amongst them. That's how she met

Doug's father who is a member of the Tjapukai tribe and an integral figure in the aboriginal rights movement.

"Somethin' about Doug though. I've never been that comfortable with him. I think he's a bit spoiled from all the attention his parents give him. Thinks real highly of himself and is convinced he'll be a movie star some day."

"That sounds like the guy I met," Billy said. "But he was a nice enough guy, offered to bring me some food after he had dinner with his parents. Said he wanted to hang out and chat, though I don't know what about."

"He probably just wanted to impress you with himself, sort of a validation of his own ego. He is a star at the dance theater, but he can't seem to get past that. They've been doing the same material for years, and, though it has merit telling the story of the Tjapukai to the tourists, I think Doug is feeling a bit stagnant. What he needs is a fresh play to perform, something with some life in it and some real characters, maybe even a little humor."

At twenty minutes before midnight Doug was released from jail after a long session of questioning. It was determined by the local authorities that he had nothing to do with the arson, so he was allowed to go home. Rebecca, Jim, and the other two men would be held for more questioning, at least until the morning.

Mr. Dolan, who was a local tourist merchant and a large contributor to the Tjapukai Dance Theater, met Doug at the jail to give him a ride home.

"Would you like to come stay up at our house Doug? Or shall I just drive you home?" Bob Dolan unlocked the passenger side of his grey sedan and gave the boy a friendly slap on the shoulder.

"I would just like to go home," Doug responded with a sigh. "I'll be okay there."

"I'm sure you will," Dolan said as he got into the driver's side of the car. "You're just about your own man anyway. I think you are growin' up real well, Doug. Lots of potential."

"Thank you," said Doug. "Your family has helped a lot over the years."

They drove for a minute or so before Dolan asked what was on his mind. "Have you ever dreamed of running your own theater, Doug?"

That comment took the contemplative young man by complete surprise and couldn't have been further from his mind. "I suppose I have," he said. "But why do you ask?"

"Well, it's like this, Doug." Dolan paused a moment. "Me and a few mates downtown have been doin' some talkin' about the dance theater. We all contribute pretty generously to its funding and we enjoy going to an occasional show, but, to be blunt, we mainly look at the theater as a way to draw people into town and into our stores. We're businessmen, Doug, and that's just how we are. The fact is that the town has grown a lot over the years, and there are many local citizens who have enjoyed the shows at the dance theater but now would like a little more diversity."

Doug didn't say a word.

"To put it bluntly again, I believe the local public is a bit bored. We all need more stimulation, that's all. We need a community center—a multiuse facility that could accommodate a wide range of productions. Everything from sporting events and rock concerts to bloody Shakespeare. Can you see it?"

Doug was definitely sitting up straighter in the car seat. He alternately looked at Bob Dolan in disbelief and then straight down the road itself. When he looked down the road, he could see it in his mind: a large community center surrounded by a parking lot full of cars and streams of people going in to see the show. But he wasn't sure what part he was supposed to play. Was he the ticket taker or the leading actor? That was when he looked back at Bob Dolan.

"But where do I fit in, Mr. Dolan?" Doug asked. "I agree it would be a wonderful thing for the town, but why are you telling me about it? What can I do to help?"

The turn indicators flashed several times as the grey sedan turned down the street where Doug's house was.

"There is no end to the possibilities for a young, enthusiastic lad like yourself. We're going to need the kind of raw talent that you have to get this whole thing off the ground." Dolan smiled as he pulled the car to a stop in front of Doug's house. "I just wanted to tell you about this so you would have something to look forward to. We're already working on the building site, and the plans for the structure should be approved by the county next week."

Doug was a little dumbstruck. He as though a dream were coming true.

"What's the matter, lad? This should be good news for you."

"Oh, it is, Mr. Dolan. Really, it is. I just didn't expect it."

"That's okay, Doug. You've had a pretty tough night. Don't worry about a thing. Just keep up the good work at the dance theater, and you'll have a fine place with us when the building is done."

"Thanks again," said Doug. "I don't know what else to say."

"Then don't say a word. Just go get some rest." Bob Dolan leaned across Doug's seat and opened the car door. "Go on, get outta here. I need some sleep myself."

When the car drove away, Doug walked into his parent's house. He suddenly felt like he had outgrown it. In the course of one night he felt as though he had matured from adolescence into full adulthood.

He glanced around the house and saw the dinner table just the way they had left it. Feeling restless, he picked up the plate that his mother had begun for the kid down at the billabong. He piled it high with heaps of leftovers and covered it with two cloth napkins.

It's probably a little ridiculous to go down there right now, Doug thought. I'm sure that kid is asleep. But I could find where he is camped and leave the food for him to find in the morning. Really, I just want to go for a walk, and this gives me a good excuse.

With his mind made up, Doug pulled the door of his parents' house closed and began the walk to the billabong. He brought a flashlight with him, but he didn't need to use it until he was all the way down to the water. Knowing right where to find the clear-water spring, it didn't take him long to locate Billy's camp, but Billy wasn't there.

Doug tried not to shine his light directly at the camp at first because he didn't want to wake Billy up; but while looking for a suitable place to leave the food, he could not help noticing that no one was there. He shined his light around the camp more boldly and decided that he was definitely in the right camp because he recognized the pack that Billy had been carrying the day before. But where was he now, in the middle of the night?

Shining his light on the heap of wood and the burnt out embers of a fire, Doug decided that the boy had been gone for several hours. Then he remembered Leonard and laughed to himself. "I wonder if he met up with that old man and got lured back to the cave for a few old stories. Oh well, no harm there; he'll be back before too long. Maybe I'll stoke up his fire a bit."

Doug began to build up a blaze and, finding the book that Billy had been reading, settled in to make himself comfortable in the young man's camp.

The flowing narrative written by Henry Lawson easily captured Doug's attention. He read each sentence with the delight of having discovered a marvelous new dessert with just the right aperitif. Never before had he read the words of an author who spoke so directly. Where had this kind of literature been at school?

Time slipped away while the young boy read. Slowly his mind was filled with the images of the story. When he felt that he could contain no more, he closed his eyes to let the fantasy take over.

He dreamed that a train pulled away from a lonely, wooden platform somewhere on the Plains of Nullarbor. An aged, white-haired aborigine man smiled a foolish grin as a lethargic donkey strained against the weight of its wagon.

Ben Ben smiled as one of the final pieces of his puzzle fell into place. He had trusted that his most current dilemma would resolve itself in the natural manner of his past experiences, but he usually had more to go on than a dream.

A dream or a long-distance, telepathic communication—the only difference Ben Ben could see was the way in which various societies viewed the topic. In Ben Ben's own way of looking at it, any dream that repeated itself to the dreamer was an obvious attempt at communication. This idea had never been proven wrong in the wide span of his life.

It was the natural progression of his life to be eating dinner at a truck stop in Brisbane with only the unfamiliar town as his destination. He had been following a most persistent dream for a little more than a week, and he knew he was getting close to the source.

At first he hadn't realized that it was Leonard who was calling him, but in the last few days he had started to hear his old friend's name in the dream along with the sounds of a dijereedoo somewhere in the distance. He listened carefully the second night as the music described a watery billabong on the east coast of the continent. Ben Ben was in Perth, on the west coast, at the time, and he had no idea why he would be called to go east. But the song of the dijereedoo is one of the most ancient sounds in the racial memory of his heritage. After a third night of the same dream he knew he had to follow it.

"It sounds like you're looking for Kuranda," said the waiter. "That's where you'll find the dance theater you're describing."

"Thank you," said Ben Ben. "I wasn't sure of the name of the town."

After more than a week and almost three thousand miles he finally had a name to look for on a map. He felt the warm glow of satisfaction that people feel when they are nearing the end of a long, hard journey.

"Kuranda? Did you say you're goin' to Kuranda?" A truck driver, two seats away at the same counter, turned to look at Ben Ben.

"Yes." Even the wise, old Aborigine had not expected this.

"Well, I'm goin' there right now," said the driver. "Got a load of frozen food to drop off by five o'clock in the morning."

"Looks like you've got yourself a ride." The waiter smiled at Ben Ben enthusiastically.

"If you are offering me a ride, I would really appreciate it." This was a stroke of luck even for Ben Ben.

"No worries, mate. Finish your meal."

Leonard poked around at the embers in his fire pit, stirring up the coals before placing more wood on them. Billy watched as the sparks crackled and popped, circling and spiraling their way to the rocky ceiling of the cave.

"Those sparks remind me of Doug," Leonard mused. "See how brightly they shine? Glowing in their magnificence, they are pulled irresistibly toward the sky, as if their fiery essence alone could place them in the company of the stars. They shine for all they are worth and, for a moment, succeed in their celestial attempts. But for them there is no escape. Spark after spark will vaingloriously surge toward the cosmos only to hit the same immovable barrier and tumble down, spent and exhausted, amid the ashes of its peers.

"Doug is the same way with his talent and desire for stardom. His boundaries are the cultural dogma inherent in the tradition of his dance. He yearns to break free of that and to express himself in a myriad of ways."

Billy stared at the flames that licked and caressed the new wood that Leonard had added. Most of the sparks that had been stirred up had now returned to the embers, with only an occasional brave meteor attempting an ascension.

"What do you mean by 'cultural dogma'?" Billy asked expressionlessly.

"Cultural dogma? Did I say that? I'm sorry, I meant no offense. The traditions of the tribal dance are integral to the legacy of their culture. I understand. I've been a part of it and seen it in action for many years. I have no bones to pick with tradition until it hinders evolution.

"That's where Doug has his problem—with evolution. He can't seem to find a way for his expressions to evolve. He is very loyal to his heritage, partly because of his parents and who they are, and partly because of the notoriety he receives through the theater. That's the way to reach him though, through the theater."

"But you say he is tired of the theater or at least with the material they provide. Why doesn't he just leave, go to Sydney, and have a go at it there? That's where I'm bound."

"Oh, no you're not." Leonard sat up straight. "You're stayin' right here in Kuranda. Don't you know you came here for a reason? All things happen for a reason. Every action has a reason, and it is within the powers of men, women, even children, to determine what that significance is."

"But, I never had any intentions of coming to Kuranda. I've had enough of small towns. I'm on my way to the city. The only reason I'm here is because this is where my last ride dropped me off."

"That's the beauty of it. Often our actions are dictated by someone else, and it is only through the powers of our own intellect that we are able to distill the intoxicating virtues."

"But, why would I want to stay in Kuranda? There's nothing for me here; I'm just setting out to see the world. I don't want to stop in my own backyard."

"The whole world is your backyard, Billy. But I understand what you are saying. You want to travel and see some of the exotic places and things that you've read about. I know you're a reader, Billy. You have the inquisitive look of a reader. And I bet you fancy yourself a bit of a writer as well, even though you come from a poor, uneducated family. Your father has been out droving for the last few years, has he not?"

"How do you know these things about me? Did I tell you and just don't remember?"

"You have a fear of being a drover yourself, don't you, Billy? As for your questions—of course I know those things about you. Subconscious expression, remember?"

"May I roll another cigarette?" Billy gestured toward the tobacco sack.

"Please do; help yourself. I'm sorry if I frighten you with the things I say," Leonard apologized again. "I just figure that I might as well call the shots as I see them. I guess when you've been around as long as I have, you begin to lose the taste for small talk. Time is of the essence when you consider the tiny span of a person's life. If I can startle someone like yourself with the things I say, if I can inspire you at your tender age, then I'm doing a positive thing.

"Great painters inspire people with their paintings, great composers through their music. I am but a thinker and a talker and a small-time carver of wood. Over the years I have come to realize that my noblest endeavor is to inspire others. To open someone else's eyes, so that they may achieve the full magnificence of their own special gifts, is truly a gift in itself.

"Take yourself, for example. We have been talking for most of the night now, and, though you didn't come here consciously seeking enlightenment, you have, through the course of our conversation, begun to view yourself in a new light. No longer are you an uneducated, country kid, but now a mature adult capable of sustaining a highly intellectual discourse. Maybe with a little more talking I can convince you of the validity of your dreams."

Billy had finished rolling his cigarette and was now pacing the room enjoying the smoke.

"Then, tell me," Billy said, "what is it that you have in mind for me?"

Rain was still coming down pretty hard from a sky that was just barely beginning to lighten with the first signs of the approaching sunrise.

"The theater," Leonard volunteered. "I believe that a good place for you to begin your illustrious writing career is in the theater. Right here in Kuranda."

"The theater?" Billy was surprised. "But, I wouldn't have any idea what to do in the theater."

"Why, you'd write plays, of course, and produce them." Once Leonard got hold of a notion, he had a talent for stringing it out plainly for all to see.

"Oh, sure. Like it's that easy." Billy was growing weary of this old man and his big talk and inflated ideas. But there was something undeniably flattering in his suggestions.

"Of course, it's that easy, Billy. Do you think it should be harder? Am I gettin' through to ya, lad? I feel like you're tunin' me out. Like maybe you're thinkin' I'm just spoutin' off; like an old whale in shallow water. But I'm here, an' I'm tellin' you, things don't have to be as hard as people make 'em out to be."

"But, I don't know how to write a play. I've never even been in a theater."

"That's wonderful!! A bonus in your favor, and you didn't even know it. You've been spared the exploitation of mass media and all its mechanical fascinations. Your appreciation of literature, and your inspiration to create, come to you on a rare level not often seen in today's over-hyped, make-a-buck world. I'm glad to make your acquaintance." Leonard bowed low and swept his right arm in a gesture of respect.

"But," stammered Billy, afraid to suddenly appear ignorant, "how does that help me write plays?"

It all came together in a flash. The old man got chills down his spine as he said, "The classics. Billy, my boy, that's it. You need to interpret the classics for the poor, befuddled masses. The Australian classics, of course. Henry Lawson, Banjo Patterson, you know, the jolly swagman camped beside the billabong. Right here in Kuranda.

"The tourists are already here to see a show. Why not give 'em another half-hour of entertainment? We could do it outside, in an amphitheater cut into the jungle. There would be no trouble with the city council; Doug's parents would swing that. Why, the two of you could start your own theater troupe in conjunction with the dance theater. It's not like you'd be competing, because each theater would offer something different. They'd still have their heritage and cultural dances, while you'd have modern interpretations of the time-tested classics.

"No one else is doing it. Your outdoor theater could be one of a kind; it might become renowned throughout the country. If your adaptations were clever and cunning enough, you might become hailed as a brilliant playwright and eventually be able to sell some of your own material. Wouldn't that be nice?"

Billy had to agree. The old man painted a pretty rosy picture. Right now, Billy's thoughts were wavering around from notion to notion, like the flickering flames about to die off and become embers. On one hand, he wanted to leave behind this crazy old man and his wild, rambling ideas, pick up his swag and go blend back into the country, just hitchhike around and see a bit of the world, not have to answer anybody's questions. But, then again, wasn't this the perfect opportunity to stay in one place and begin a career, to have a chance to create a nice life that would be fitting for a wife and a family, a chance to step out of the footsteps of his father and the droving life toward which they led?

"There is a certain therapy in movement." Leonard interrupted the young man's thoughts. "A lot can be said for the man who can get up and walk away from a problem. A complete change in the pattern of one's life—the daily routine as well as the physical scenery—is essential for the evolution of one's soul. But I don't think this is your problem. Finding a routine and rooting yourself to a commitment—now that is something difficult for you.

"It was for me, too. I've spent most of my life drifting from one place to the next, job to job, manual labor and artistic endeavors, but searching all the while. I didn't even know what I was searching for; I just knew I wasn't finding it.

"More than sixty years I've stumbled around on the face of this planet, searching for something that I carried with me every step of the way. Peace and contentment are what we're all looking for, and I'm tellin' you, just like a preacher, that it is all inside yourself.

"I have had moments of ecstatic joy pumpin' gas an' changin' tires for an offbeat, one-lane track in the outback for no other reason except the recognition of how bored I had been at a big-time exhibit of my own art the week before in Sydney. I've been so lonely I've cried to the pitiless stars at night, wondering why I couldn't settle down and fall in love. Simple fact was, I can see years later, that I never really loved myself, so there was no possible way that I could love someone else.

"I held ideals of myself in front of my nose like a carrot in front of a mule. I told myself that as soon as I became the way I wanted myself to be, then all the rest of the loose ends of my life would come together. You don't want to fall into that trap, lad. Not if you can help it."

A few minutes passed.

"Are you really that sad? Are you trying to tell me that life has passed you by?" Billy was concerned.

"No, I don't feel that way anymore. I made my peace a few years back. Now I just try and express it to others. I mainly do it with my dijereedoo, as I'm doing with Ben Ben. The dijereedoo has a magic all its own, capable of telling heroic sagas as well as tales of disenchantment and woe. Anything I can dream up, I can express through my dijereedoo. Usually I tailor the melody to fit my audience. With you it was easy; you are very much like myself."

"But how did you know I was around here or that I would hear your music?" Billy still didn't get it.

"Listen to the world around you, lad. It told me of your passing."

Light from the first rays of dawn filtered its way through the ground mist, fog, and slowly departing rain clouds. Another day was commencing in the rainforests of Queensland, and soon the creatures that inhabited this small billabong would set about the routine of their existence.

"I remember an image," said Leonard, standing up and extending his hand as a way to ease Billy's imminent departure. "You were thinking of it just before we met."

Billy shook the old man's hand with sincere friendship.

"You had been listening to my music—which had just stopped—and you were imagining the whole world hanging by a slender thread with a man below holding a giant disposable lighter. The cataclysmic incinerator was threatening life as you knew it. Then my music started again, and everything was okay. The constant rhythmic roll of the universe was restored." The wise old man held, for a moment longer, the hand of the youth. "Who do you suppose that man was, if not yourself? Was it me? Am I the bringer of such a radical change in your life that you were afraid of me? Time itself ticks away, and so does life. Can you really afford to stay the same?"

Billy's eyes pulled away from the penetrating stare of his new friend. He looked around the cave and was comforted by the carved, wooden images that now seemed familiar.

"Go now," Leonard said. "Enough for one night. I can see your heart. I'll be here when you need me."

Something about Kuranda seemed vaguely familiar to Ben Ben even in the predawn darkness. Maybe it was just the vividness of the dream he had been having while he dozed in the cab of the truck.

"Usually I don't let people sleep while I'm driving," said the truck driver. "It makes me tired and I can't let that happen. I almost pulled over to toss you out, but some weird notion got a hold o' me, and I just let you sleep. I guess you're just lucky."

Ben Ben regarded the man for a moment.

"What can I say except thank you?"

"That'll do," said the driver. "I hope the rest of your day is a lucky as it started."

"Right, then. G'day, mate."

Ben Ben walked away from the truck and around the corner of the building to the front of a grocery store. The store was closed, and it looked like the rest of Kuranda was sleeping as well. It did not take long for Ben Ben to find his way around town. Before ten minutes had passed, he was standing in front of the Tjapukai Dance Theater.

Closed and dark though it was, the dance theater filled Ben Ben with a sense of welcome. He knew with the wisdom of his soul that something meaningful had brought him here. Maybe the morning would bring some answers.

Billy took his time walking back to his camp; he was in no hurry and planned to just go to sleep when he got there. His head was swirling with thoughts, and he really had no clear idea which way to go with any of them.

In the distant background he heard Leonard's dijereedoo and smiled at the familiarity of it. Then he saw smoke rising from a fire that he assumed exhausted itself hours ago. Hurrying a little, he came into full view of the camp and saw Doug leaning against his pack, asleep. He also saw the big pile of food on the plate next to him.

"Hey mate, what's up?" Billy said softly as he walked in to his camp. He didn't want to startle the sleeper, but he did want him to wake up.

"Oh, you're back." Doug sat up from his slumbering position. "I brought you some food, but you weren't here. So, I stoked up your fire and waited a while." Doug stood up and stretched. "It started raining, and I didn't want to walk home, so I just stayed and stayed. You were gone all night."

"I know," said Billy. "I'm pretty bushed. That food sure looks good."

"Here, help yourself." Doug passed the plate and Billy took a piece of cold, fried chicken.

"This is good. Thanks."

While eating the chicken, Billy put a few pieces of wood on the fire to get it going again. "I met this strange man," he said between bites. "He lives in a cave."

"Right, that's Leonard. I know him. He is a bit out there, but a decent chap all-in-all."

"He said he knew you also," said Billy. "We had the most intense talk, and by the end of it he had designed some pretty lofty plans for you and me."

"The two of us?" Doug responded. "What kind of plans did he have for you and me?"

"It all involved the dance theater and me writing plays and producing them with you."

"That is incredible. You wouldn't believe the offer I had tonight." Doug began to explain the chain of events that occurred since he had left Billy the day before. "And now, here we are, after both having such intensely revealing experiences. I wonder what it all means." Doug was mystified.

"I think it means that you and I are destined to do great things together," said Billy. "Either that, or we're just both in the right place at the same time."

"Well, I'm glad you stumbled in to town. It's nice to meet you, partner." Doug put out his hand and shook Billy's. As they both laughed, a kookaburra in the jungle joined in with its happy, frivolous melody.

When Ben Ben heard the sounds of the dijereedoo he knew that he was not dreaming, even though he had been resting beneath a comfortable tree in front of the theater. He stood up when he first heard the instrument. Instinctively he followed the music down the hill to the billabong, but then it seemed to fade away. Without being sure which way the enticing melody had come from,

Ben Ben naturally followed the trail further down the hill. Soon he saw smoke from a fire.

"Excuse me," Ben Ben said to Doug as he approached the camp. "Was that you playing the dijereedoo a moment ago?"

"No, it wasn't," replied the young dancer, turning to look at the stranger.

"It must've been Leonard," Billy said.

"Leonard? Do you know Leonard?" asked Ben Ben.

"Of course we know Leonard. Everybody around here knows Leonard." Doug rolled his eyes at Ben Ben and then looked sideways at Billy. "This guy looks just like the guy in my dream."

"What dream?" said Billy, a little confused.

"The dream I was having just before you woke me up. But, wait a minute, who are you?" Doug turned back toward the stranger.

"My name is Ben Ben, and I have come a long way to see Leonard. Do you know where he is?"

"I'm right here," Leonard said as he stepped from behind a tree. "Greetings, old friend." The two old men hugged each other in a long embrace. "I'm glad you've come."

"Now just hold on," said Billy. "How did you get here, Leonard?"

"Well," the old musician said with a brief pause, "I began to play my dijereedoo after you left, but I couldn't shake the feeling that Doug might be down here waiting for you. I was a little anxious to know how the two of you would get along, so I

81

decided to see for myself. Then, to pile a paradox on top of a coincidence, I saw Ben Ben on the trail in front of me. One part of me wanted to rush ahead and talk to my old friend, but another part of me wanted to secretly witness the meeting I've waited years to see." Leonard looked cautiously from face to face.

"I'm afraid you've lost me," Ben Ben admitted. "What is this meeting you've waited years to see?"

"This one, right here, right now." Leonard chuckled nervously. "For years I've wanted to introduce you to your son."

"My son?" Ben Ben exclaimed. "I don't have a son!"

"Oh, but you do." Leonard was serious. "You are the true father of Doug, this young man right here."

"You're a crazy old man!" shouted the dark-skinned dancer. "My father is a brave and respected man, not some stranger."

"I know it is hard for you to understand, but let me try and explain." Leonard reached out his hand to comfort the young man, but Doug pushed away the friendly gesture.

"Maybe you should try and explain this—to both of us." Ben Ben was trying to sound firm.

Billy was not sure what any of it meant.

A tense silence prevailed as each person in the group waited for the outcome.

At last Leonard began. "Let me start by saying to you, Doug, that your mother has wanted to tell you for years, but she has been afraid of the trouble it would cause. I have wanted to tell my friend, Ben Ben, but I haven't said anything until now because of my respect for your mother, Rebecca."

"Rebecca? I remember Rebecca!" A light turned on inside Ben Ben's face.

"You should remember her," Leonard continued, "although it has been a long time—seventeen years—since your short, but intense affair. Don't you remember the little town of Kuranda? Back in the last days that you and I travelled together, we stopped here for a short while. You and Rebecca met at a rally, and I couldn't separate the two of you for three days. She was beautiful and I loved her as much as you did, but she loved you."

Everyone was listening.

"Then, suddenly, you wanted to leave town. So I went with you but only for a few weeks, then we also split up. Do you remember that?"

"Yes, I do," Ben Ben said meekly.

"After you and I split up, I came back to Kuranda to see Rebecca. She was already involved with Jim—and I've always thought that maybe it was because of Jim that you wanted to leave—but she told me that she had missed her menstrual period and thought she might be pregnant with your child. I didn't know where you were going, and it was all getting too heavy for me in Kuranda, so I left for a walkabout. Rebecca married Jim and gave birth to Doug."

No one said a word. Ben Ben and Doug looked long at each other, trying to imagine if it were possible that they were related.

"I have watched the boy grow up. Rebecca and I both believe you are his father, Ben Ben. Doug is very much like you." Leonard turned away from the scrutinizing gaze of the father and son. Again the silence prevailed.

After a while Leonard spoke again. "Maybe I was wrong to bring you all together like this, but I believe the time is right. The circle is coming together for all of us, just as it does for everyone eventually. There are things you need to share with your son, Ben Ben. He has been cheated out of his true heritage. He has been stifled here because he doesn't yet realize his true totem. I believe it is a laughing, singing kookaburra, just the same as yours, but he has been trapped here. You can teach him so much. Relate to him the joys you've known so that he might know them also. He is your son; you can do at least that much for him."

"But I don't want to pick up and leave with a total stranger," said Doug.

"You don't have to," Leonard emphasized. "Just listen to him and learn from him. It may help you express yourself better when you start your contemporary theater with Billy."

Everyone turned to look at Billy. The questions between Doug and Ben Ben were forgotten for just a moment as Leonard continued. "This brings me around in a full circle to Billy's purpose in all of this. I believe he would make a most excellent partner in a theater for the marvelous reason that he has been born into an extremely rare Dreaming, a Billabong Dreaming—a mental billabong, if you follow me. An intellectual wellspring where expressive thought becomes truly limitless."

"I can see how all of this could come together," said Billy, wearing the expression of a visionary on his face. "If Ben Ben can stick around for a while, then maybe we can work this into something. Can he stay with you in your cave, Leonard?"

"I don't see why not. How about it, Ben Ben?" Leonard looked quizzically at his old friend.

"I'm in no hurry to leave," the new father responded. "But what about Rebecca and her husband, Jim? How are they going to take all of this?"

Everyone turned toward Doug. "I really don't know what to say," he mumbled a little aimlessly.

"Rebecca will be okay with it," said Leonard. "It may even be a bit of a relief for her. But I am a little concerned for Jim. He thinks you are his son, Doug, and that is going to hurt."

"But I don't want to hurt him," Doug pleaded. "He's the only dad I've ever known. Can't we just forget about all of this? Why don't you just go away?" The confused young man looked scornfully at his biological father.

"This is very hard for me, too," said Ben Ben, knowing it was time for him to speak up. "But, if all of this is true, then we need to confront it. It's no good trying to run away from the truth." He paused to gather his strength and to look at his son. "For most of my life I've wandered around the country, reluctant to take on the heritage of my father. My songline led me far and wide, but rarely did it lead me home. This is the habit of a kookaburra, and it may be a mixed blessing for you. It may seem that I've spent my life in a frivolous way, but I've always been searching—searching for answers and an overall meaning to my life."

Ben Ben's eyes squinted as though he held back a tear, and then his expression changed to one of profound understanding. "Maybe you were the elusive answer that I could never quite grasp. I was never ready for the tribal leadership role that I was born into, but maybe you are. Because of your mixed heritage, you may be able to transcend the cultural barriers that always opposed me. You have the gift of expressive dance; that is a happy and very powerful way to communicate. You may be able to use it to champion the cause of not only our tribal concerns but the concerns of the Aborigine people across the country. Your dance theater could be much larger and more widely accepted than you ever dreamed—and I can help; I know the concerns of the people."

Now it was Leonard's turn to speak again. He held one hand up as if he could hang on to the moment. "I believe there is a lesson for all of us in this, and that is to follow our intuition. That inner voice which we all hear is trying to guide us on the correct path in our lives. We are lucky to have it all come together like this—it may fulfill all of our dreams, and we may inspire other people to fulfill theirs. It remains to be seen. Maybe even Jim has another part to play. He knows the concerns of the people pretty well himself. We just need to bring it all together."

"I'm willing to try," said Billy.

"So am I." Ben Ben looked hopefully at his son and marveled at this new opportunity to see Rebecca again. "I wonder what your mother will feel about me."

"I don't know," Doug responded.

"Maybe we should all go back to my place," Leonard suggested. "I can make some breakfast, and it will give us a chance to relax and get to know each other a little."

They all appreciated this idea and quickly put sand on Billy's fire and began helping him carry his things to Leonard's cave. The last bit of smoke from the extinguished fire drifted high above the jungle canopy and mingled with the sunlight of the coming day.

The day looked hopeful and promising to everyone as they walked away from Billy's camp. Somehow the pieces of each one of their puzzles looked like they might actually fit together, but the picture was not yet complete. It was not until they left the main trail and began scrambling over the boulders that Doug heard his mother calling his name.

"Is that Rebecca?" Ben Ben asked Leonard.

"That's my mom." Doug looked over his shoulder with a worried expression.

"I think she's comin' down the main trail," Billy estimated.

"Douglas! Where are you?" The woman sounded like she was on the verge of hysteria.

"Over here, Mom!" The dancer leaped easily onto a boulder and waved his arms for his mother to see.

She was very close and broke into a run at the sight of him. Doug jumped down from the rock and caught her in his arms as she burst upon the scene.

"What's the matter, Mom?" he said soothingly.

"Oh, Doug," she cried as she buried her head against his chest. "It's so terrible."

"*What* is, Mom? Please tell me. Where is Dad?" Doug looked up the trail anxiously. He saw Mr. Dolan and Officer Hardy approaching.

"Oh, Doug, I'm so sorry." Rebecca pulled her head up and for the first time noticed Billy, Leonard, and, last of all, Ben Ben. It took only a moment for the recognition to sink in.

"Why are you sorry, Mom? What happened?" Doug was looking at her, and she had to struggle not to look back at Ben Ben.

"Oh, Doug." Rebecca was torn and confused. "Your father has been killed." She began sobbing again.

"Oh, Momma," Doug held her tighter. "But how? And who?" he cried.

"We are looking into that right now," Officer Hardy said as he put a hand on Doug's shoulder. "Right now we have one of the prisoners who shared his cell; we think he did it, but we don't know how he got the knife or why he used it against your father."

Mr. Dolan stood a little to the side and looked at Leonard and Ben Ben instead of the mother and child. Perhaps he was wondering why these two other men were there witnessing this exchange.

Ben Ben looked at Mr. Dolan and then at Leonard. He tried to read the expression on the face of his friend, but his own heart ached for the loss Rebecca and Doug were going through. As he had done all his life, Ben Ben followed his instincts when they urged him to walk over and embrace the weeping mother and their child.

"I am very sorry for both of you. I hope I can help." He put his big arms around each of them and pulled them close.

Mr. Dolan raised his eyebrows and Officer Hardy stepped back a pace, but Leonard and Billy could only stare, as if in a Dreamtime, as Doug and his mom sought solace in the arms of a stranger.

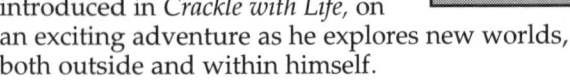